For two special sisters – Abigail and Imogen

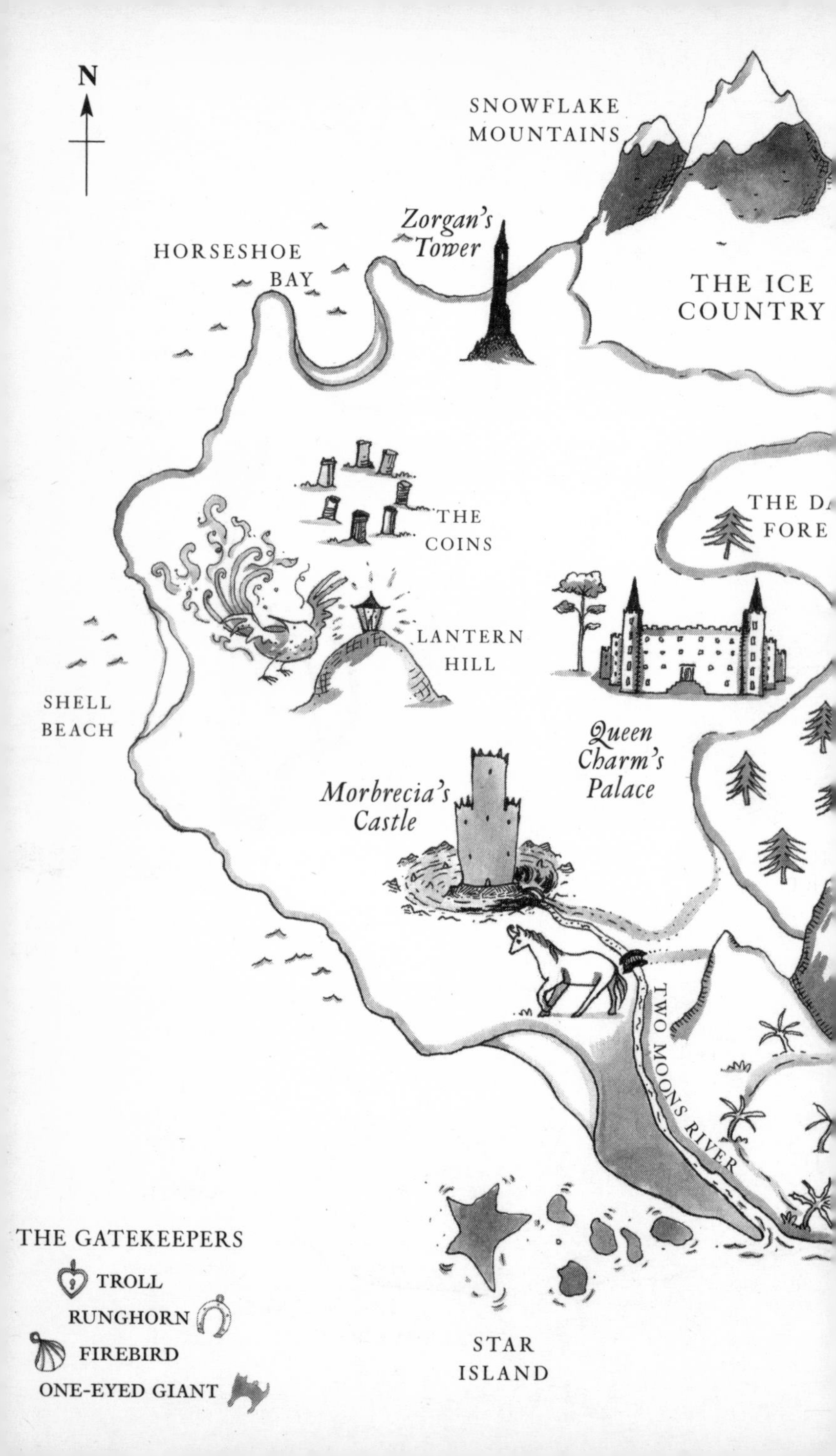
N
SNOWFLAKE MOUNTAINS
Zorgan's Tower
HORSESHOE BAY
THE ICE COUNTRY
THE COINS
LANTERN HILL
SHELL BEACH
Queen Charm's Palace
Morbrecia's Castle
TWO MOONS RIVER
STAR ISLAND
THE GATEKEEPERS
TROLL
RUNGHORN
FIREBIRD
ONE-EYED GIANT

CHARMSEEKERS: BOOK FOUR

A Tale of Two Sisters

Georgie Adams

Illustrated by Gwen Millward

Orion
Children's Books

First published in Great Britain in 2008
by Orion Children's Books
Reissued 2011 by Orion Children's Books
a division of the Orion Publishing Group Ltd
Orion House
5 Upper St Martin's Lane
London WC2H 9EA
An Hachette Livre UK Company

1 3 5 7 9 10 8 6 4 2

The Orion Publishing Group's policy is to use papers that are natural, renewable and recyclable products and made from wood grown in sustainable forests. The logging and manufacturing processes are expected to conform to the environmental regulations of the country of origin.

ISBN 978 1 44400292 8

Printed and bound in the UK by CPI Mackays, Chatham ME5 8TD

www.orionbooks.co.uk

KARISMA
CAPE
CAT
HEARTMOOR
CLOVER FIELDS
DOLPHIN BAY
MOUNT
ORTUNA
The Silver Pool
KEY
POINT
SWAMPS
JUNGLE
MERMAID
ROCK
BUTTERFLY BAY

The Thirteen Charms of Karisma

When Charm became queen of Karisma, the wise and beautiful Silversmith made her a precious gift. It was a bracelet. On it were fastened thirteen silver amulets, which the Silversmith called "charms", in honour of the new queen.

It was part of Karisma law. Whenever there was a new ruler the Silversmith made a special gift, to help them care for the world they had inherited. And this time it was a bracelet. She told Queen Charm it was magical because the charms held the power to control the forces of nature and keep everything in balance. She must take the greatest care of them. As long as she, and she alone, had possession of the charms all would be well.

And so it was until the bracelet was stolen by a spider, and fell into the hands of Zorgan, the magician. Then there was chaos.

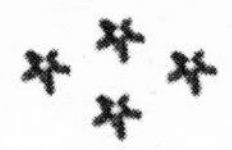

The Silversmith gazes up at the breathtaking beauty of the heavens. Somewhere out there in the infinity of the universe is her Charmseeker, Sesame Brown. Yet, despite the oceans of space that separate them, she feels close to her seeker – feels a bond between them which will endure, long after the quest is over.

She turns to look at the thirteen magic candles. Ten still burn. The Silversmith is thankful that the bracelet, heart, horseshoe and shell charms are safe with Sesame. How she longs for the day when all the charms are united!

Meanwhile, there is the problem of Morbrecia. If she is after the charms, she'll stop at nothing to prevent Sesame finding them. And Zorgan is out to make trouble for everyone! Something has to be done to protect her Charmseeker. But what? Tomorrow she will go and see Charm . . .

One

Charm should not have been surprised to hear that Morbrecia might have stolen her bracelet. The two sisters had been rivals since childhood. Nevertheless, it hurt Charm to think of Morbrecia's treachery. Recently her suspicions had been aroused by something the Silversmith had said. Since then Charm had barely slept a wink. So when the Silversmith came to see her, they spent the afternoon talking. Charm's maid, Ozina, brought them a tray of tissam,* and poured cups of the fragrant tea from an elegant silver pot.

* *

Tissam – a tea made from the dried leaves of the tissam shrub

"My own sister!" said Charm, when Ozina had left the room. "How *could* she betray me?"

"We've no proof it *was* Morbrecia, Your Majesty," said the Silversmith cautiously. "There's nothing to link her with the spider. Even if it's true, I think Zorgan tricked Morbrecia into stealing your bracelet—"

"Zorgan again!" exclaimed Charm. "That balam* magician is the cause of all our troubles. Anyway, it doesn't excuse Morbrecia. She shouldn't have trusted him. Though," she added ruefully, "I admit there was a time when I thought Zorgan could do no wrong."

The Silversmith raised an eyebrow.

"When?" she asked.

"Surely you remember?" replied Charm, refilling their cups. "I was only four the first time I saw Zorgan. I was at Morbrecia's sixth birthday party and he gave a magic show. It was a wonderful surprise."

"How out of character!" observed the Silversmith dryly. "I can't imagine Zorgan doing a good turn."

"Quite," agreed Charm. "Anyway he performed some fantastic tricks. I remember he conjured a doll

* *

* **Balam** – cursed, an angry exclamation

from thin air. It looked just like Morbrecia! It became her favourite and she took it everywhere. I believe she still has it."

"Hm," murmured the Silversmith, a faraway look in her eyes. A worrying thought had occurred to her. Then, catching Charm's puzzled expression she said: "It's nothing. Please go on."

"My sister and I thought Zorgan was marvellous," said Charm. "We were delighted when our parents made him Court Magician."

The Silversmith recalled the day King Orin and Queen Amilla had made the announcement. "Your parents must have trusted Zorgan," she said.

"Yes," said Charm. "He couldn't do enough to please them. From the start he encouraged Morbrecia to take an interest in magic."

"Because he knew she'd be queen?" suggested the Silversmith. "He saw a chance to influence her."

Charm nodded.

"I suppose so," she said. "But everything changed on my seventh birthday, when Quilla came to see my father—"

"I know of the fairy, Quilla," said the Silversmith. "She lives backwards, if you see what I mean. She grows younger with age, and she knows the future."

"Ah!" said Charm. "That would explain it. Quilla knew something and came to warn him."

"I'm intrigued," said the Silversmith.

"Ozina told me everything," said Charm, in a conspiratorial tone. "I still rely on her to tell me what goes on around here. I know how she loves to gossip! Officer Dork was on duty that day and he told her . . .

"I took this fairy, Quilla, to the king and queen, right? In a bit of a hurry, she was. Said it was urgent. Their Majesties weren't too pleased about seeing her, 'cause they were going to Princess Charm's party. But she was very persistent, so they agreed. Well, I was backing and bowing out of the room when King Orin says, "Wait, Dork!" So I stood there. Heard it all, I did.

"What's this all about?" asks His Majesty.

"I have seen the future," says Quilla. "Your daughter Morbrecia will never be queen."

"WHAT!" shouts His Maj. banging his fist on the throne.

"How dare you suggest such a thing," says the Queen.

But the fairy doesn't budge. "You must believe me," she says. "Charm will be queen of Karisma. You must tell the princess her fate, without delay . . ."

"My poor father!" said Charm. "He told me later he didn't know what to do for the best. But he believed in Quilla. She was a good fairy. He hoped to find the right time before telling us both."

"He knew how upset Morbrecia would be," said the Silversmith.

"Precisely," said Charm. "But Zorgan found out and spoiled everything. He did something dreadful at my party."

"What?" asked the Silversmith.

Charm leaned towards her and said, "I thought I was going to die!"

Two

It was late afternoon, the day of the pop concert. Sesame had been trying out some new nail varnish and had painted her nails sparkling pink, yellow and green. While she waited for them to dry, she gazed out of her window, wondering what to wear. She could hardly believe that in only a few hours she'd be meeting her favourite girl band, Crystal Chix. It was like a dream come true. Her tummy flipped, just thinking about it.

Her dad, Nic, was a press photographer. He'd been booked for a photo shoot at the concert, and had three free tickets. So he was taking Sesame and two of her friends. Before the show, they were all going backstage to meet the band!

Sesame was still daydreaming, when she spotted Chips in the garden. He was stalking a bird! Horrified, she watched as he crouched in the long grass – ears flat, body quivering, eyes fixed on a robin.

"Chips!" she yelled. "No!"

Her warning didn't deter him and before she could shout *Shoo!* – he sprang. But to her relief (and Chips' fury) the robin flew into an apple tree, where it sat on a branch, singing. Just then Sesame's mobile jingled. It was a text from Gemma, and there was a

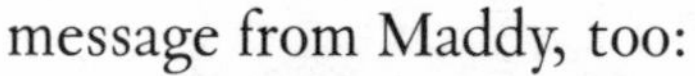

message from Maddy, too:

Sesame smiled. It was going to be fun. She'd be with her best friend Maddy Webb and crazy Gemma Green who was always doing wicked things. Sesame sent replies:

As she switched off her mobile, she heard Lossy calling her. Sesame jumped downstairs two at a time and found her gran in the kitchen, preparing a salad.

"Could you feed Chips and Pins, please?" said Lossy. "Then we'll have tea. Your dad should be here soon."

"I'm SO excited," said Sesame, dancing to the cupboard for cat food. "I couldn't eat a thing."

"You must eat *something*," insisted Lossy. "Goodness, look at your nails!"

Sesame waggled her fingers.

"Funky!" she said.

"Frightful," said Lossy, with a smile.

While Sesame shook biscuits into bowls, Pins watched her, purring.

"Where's Chips?" asked Lossy. "It's not like him to be late."

"He's probably in the garden," said Sesame. "I saw him stalking a bird."

She went outside to look. At first there was no sign of him, then she heard a pitiful *MIAOW!* Chips had climbed into the apple tree, and no amount of coaxing from Sesame could get him down.

"I'll fetch a ladder," said Lossy, "or you'll be there all night."

Climbing the ladder was easy. The difficult part was persuading Chips to let go of the branch. He clung on with his claws, hissed, spat, and yowled. Chips refused to move but Sesame wouldn't give up either! She stepped off the ladder and wriggled along

the bough. It was then she felt it sway. She heard the leaves rustling in the breeze, saw their shadows fluttering like butterflies in the afternoon sun . . .

Sesame felt wobbly and wrapped her arms tightly around the scratchy bark. A glint of sunlight struck the bell on Chips' collar, and silvery stars danced before her eyes! For a split-second she felt herself falling. What was happening? Had she found a way into Karisma . . . ?

MIAOW! Chips' wail jolted Sesame back in an instant. She reached out her arm, grabbed him and brought him safely down. A few minutes later he was happily eating from his bowl, as if nothing unusual had happened.

While Sesame helped Lossy set the table, she thought about the weird, muzzy feeling she'd experienced in the tree. She felt disappointed about *not* finding herself back in Karisma, but maybe there was a reason? She was still puzzling about it when her dad came in, waving three backstage passes for the concert.

Thoughts of Karisma flew out of her head, and all she could think about was meeting the Crystal Chix!

* * * *

When Sesame and Nic arrived at the SuperDome, hundreds of excited fans were queuing outside. Nic drove to the back of the stadium and parked the car at Gate 4, where Maddy and Gemma were waiting.

"Hi!" cried Sesame, hurrying to meet them.

The girls hugged and spent a few minutes chatting excitedly, admiring each other's amazing outfits. Sesame had eventually decided on a white jacket, miniskirt and silvery leggings; she'd put on her favourite chain and locket too. Maddy wore a zebra-striped dress over skinny jeans and Gemma looked fabulous in a leopard-print top, pink shorts and boots.

"Look, I made these for us," said Gemma, fishing in her bag and producing three matching friendship bracelets. She'd plaited silky threads in pink – the Crystal Chix' favourite colour.

"Wow!" said Sesame, slipping hers on. "It's fab."

"Yeah, thanks Gemma," said Maddy. "We look soooo cool! We'll be friends for ever!" Gemma was pleased. She knew Maddy and Sesame were *best* friends, but it was great they made her feel special too. It was going to be such fun tonight.

"Celebs, here we come!" she said, and they joined Nic at the gate.

The official had checked Nic's passes and was waving them through.

"Come on," said Nic. "Time to meet the stars!"

The SuperDome was huge. Backstage were lots of dressing rooms, with the performers' names pinned to the doors.

"Here we are," said Nic.

Sesame, Maddy and Gemma gave squeals of delight.

Nic knocked on the door, and it was opened by a tall girl wearing a shimmering pink tunic. She had spiky blonde hair and a dazzling smile.

"You must be Nic," she said. "We've been expecting you. "I'm Crystal. Meet Kory and Riva."

After Sesame, Maddy and Gemma had been introduced they all chatted away to the band. The girls were really friendly. Nic checked his watch. He'd allowed about forty minutes for the photo shoot, before the show began.

"Better get started," he said.

"Okay," said Crystal. "Follow me."

She led the way onto a vast stage, swarming with technicians checking lights and equipment. As they passed a dry-ice machine, they walked through a cloud of mist, coloured green by a spotlight.

"Perfect!" said Nic. "Hold it, right there."

The girls watched while Nic photographed the band. The Crystal Chix posed this way and that, until Riva smiled at Sesame and beckoned the girls to join them.

Sesame was in a daze of happiness. As she linked arms with Maddy and Gemma, she felt her necklace tingle, but she was too excited to think about it. Next moment they were standing with the Crystal Chix, swathed in a green, chilly mist.

"Right," said Nic. "SMILE!"

The camera *flashed!* Sesame, Maddy and Gemma blinked. A thousand pinpricks of light danced before their eyes. Sesame felt the ground drop away, as if a trapdoor had opened beneath her. She held onto Maddy and Gemma.

Now they were twisting . . . spiralling . . . spinning in a velvety void of darkness, falling through the vastness of time and space towards Karisma.

Three

Charm's last word hung like a thundercloud in the air.

"Die?" said the Silversmith. "How?"

The queen wandered round the room. Memories of that fateful afternoon came flooding back.

"It had started off so well," she began. "My friends and Morbrecia came. There was a treasure hunt in the maze and we all got lost! But *I* was the one who found the treasure. It was in a pot of flowers—"

"Yes, but what happened?" asked the Silversmith. She was impatient for Charm to get on with the story.

"Cook had baked a splendid cake," said Charm, determined not to miss anything out. "My parents arrived in time to see me blow out the candles. I could tell they were upset about something."

"No wonder," said the Silversmith. "They had just been talking to Quilla. What happened next?"

"Zorgan's magic show," said Charm. She felt a shiver down her spine. "Everything was fine until the last trick . . ."

"Your Royal Highness, to end the show I have a very special treat for you. Look, I have pictures of seven creatures. You shall become the one you choose. My spell will last for as long as it takes to burn a candle."

Clever Zorgan, thought the Silversmith. He knew the young princess would be fascinated.

"First, Zorgan shuffled the pictures like a pack of cards," Charm said. "Then he asked me to take one from the top. When I looked, I saw it was the bird."

"So you didn't *choose* it," observed the Silversmith.

Charm nodded.

"You're right," she said. "But I didn't think about it at the time. I was much too excited! Zorgan lit a candle. I held my breath. Then he said some magic words and waved his wand. Next thing I knew I was the prettiest little swiftwing.*

I went flying round the room and when I grew tired, I perched on a chair to rest. It was then I noticed Zorgan and Morbrecia. They were whispering together."

* *

* **Swiftwing** – emerald and crimson hummingbird. The swiftwing has amazing hearing. It can detect the sound of a beetle, crawling underground!

"I have bad news, Morbrecia. I've discovered Charm is to be queen. Not you! The fairy Quilla has seen the future. Your father has agreed. You shall never be queen of Karisma."

"No! That can't be true. *I'm* the eldest daughter. *I* should be queen!"

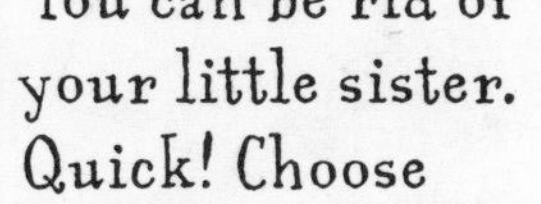

"Of course you should, Morbrecia. And I have a plan. You can be rid of your little sister. Quick! Choose this card. I'll change you into a great big CAT! Then you'll have some fun. Stalk the bird and KILL her!"

"Oh!" exclaimed the Silversmith, appalled by such a wicked plan.

"I was terrified," said Charm. "But there was nothing I could do. In an instant Morbrecia became a horrid, hissing cat. Of course I tried to fly away but my wings felt strangely heavy. She fixed her eyes on me and POUNCED! It all happened so fast. I couldn't escape the swipe of her paw. I felt her claws tearing at my throat, jaws open, her teeth . . .

"Then I heard my father shout, 'NO!' And he blew the candle out."

Charm was shaking and the colour had drained from her cheeks. The Silversmith waited for her to recover.

"And Zorgan?" she ventured, after a while. "What happened to him?"

"My father banished him from the court," said Charm. "We never saw him again. We were told he'd travelled north and was practising Dark Magic in his tower."

The Silversmith already knew of Zorgan's whereabouts. "How was Morbrecia?" she asked.

"It was the beginning of all our troubles," said Charm. "From that day on we were bitter rivals. I'm afraid Morbrecia will stop at nothing to find the charms. She is determined to rule Karisma!"

Four

They landed on an enormous boot. From the size of it Sesame supposed that it belonged to a person of gigantic proportions. When the boot suddenly rose into the air and crashed down with a

thud,

Sesame felt fairly sure the owner was wearing it. Maddy and Gemma had been clinging to a bootlace, until the moment when the boot thudded down. Then all three slid over the toecap and were deposited,

thump,

thump,

bump,

onto a cold flagstone floor.

"Oooooof!"

Gemma and Maddy went sprawling.

"Ow!" cried Sesame, landing on her bottom.

"Wha-what happened?" asked Gemma, in a daze. "Where are we?"

"Karisma!" chorused Sesame and Maddy.

But Gemma was none the wiser. They got up and brushed themselves down. They appeared to be standing in a vast room, full of jumbo-sized furniture. And from somewhere overhead, a voice was bellowing like a bull:

"Outworlders! As if I haven't got enough trouble. What d'you want?"

The girls craned their necks to see who had spoken.

Out of the boots grew two colossal legs, which supported the massive body and head of a man; as far as they could make out, the monstrous being appeared to have only one eye. He looked simply terrifying.

"Hi!" shouted Sesame bravely. "I'm Sesame Brown. And these are my friends Maddy and Gemma. We're Charmseekers."

"CHARMSEEKERS!"

boomed the giant. "Why didn't you say?"

"Duh. She just *did*," muttered Maddy.

"Ssh!" said Sesame. "He might hear."

"Charmseekers?" whispered Gemma, utterly bemused. "What are they?"

"Tell you later," promised Sesame.

With a groan, the ginormous man suddenly sat down on a chair.

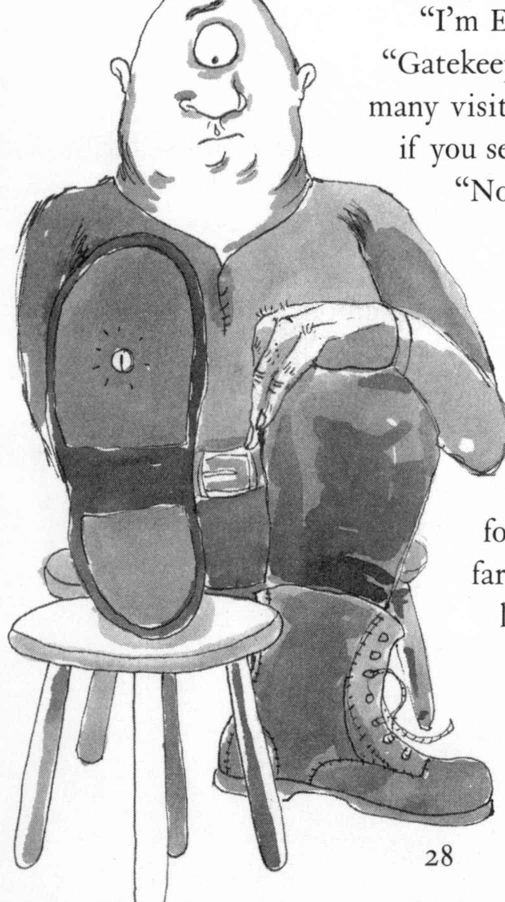

"I'm Etok," he said gruffly. "Gatekeeper Four. Don't get many visitors. Bit off the map, if you see what I mean?"

"Not really," said Sesame politely. "Where are we?"

"Cape Cat," said Etok, pointing to a large map on the wall. Sesame and Maddy looked and found Cape Cat in the far north of Karisma. It looked a remote and desolate place.

"Bet we won't find a charm here," said Maddy doubtfully.

Sesame wasn't so easily put off. She loved a challenge. "But if there *is* one," she said brightly, "Sesame Brown will track it down!"

Meanwhile Gemma, who'd been gawping at Etok, spotted something sticking out of the sole of his boot.

"Er, excuse me," she said. "I think you've trodden on a nail."

Etok leaned forward and Gemma found herself eyeball to eyeball with him. It was like looking into a goldfish bowl, without any fish in it.

"N-n-nail. B-b-boot," she stammered, wishing now she hadn't said anything. To her immense relief Etok smiled, revealing teeth as big as tombstones.

"Quisto!"* he exclaimed. "*That's* what it was! Been hurtin' for ages. Couldn't reach it, see?"

Straight away Sesame offered to help.

"Let's try and pull it out," she said. She stood on tiptoe to reach it, but she couldn't.

"We need a ladder," said Maddy.

Just then Gemma noticed some books on the floor. They were the biggest she'd ever seen.

"What about those?" she suggested.

"Okay," said Maddy. "Let's pile them up."

The three friends spent a while heaving thick volumes, one on top of the other. When they'd built steps high enough, Sesame took hold of the nail with

* *

* **Quisto** – an exclamation of surprise

both hands, Maddy gripped her round the waist and Gemma held onto Maddy. They pulled and pulled, until *Oooooof!* the nail came out – and they all tumbled backwards.

Etok sighed with relief and thanked the girls many times. When Sesame said they must go, Etok opened a huge door.

"You must return before the stroke of four," he said, pointing to the gatehouse clock. "Don't be late."

Five

"I'm curious about the doll," said the Silversmith. Ever since Charm had mentioned the doll Zorgan had given to Morbrecia, disturbing thoughts had been darting like minnows through her head.

"Let me see," said Charm. "What did Morbrecia call it? El-something. El-mo! That's it. I remember Elmo got me into trouble once or twice."

"You?" queried the Silversmith. "How?"

"I was about nine," said Charm. "Morbrecia and I had a new governess. Albina Trum. Before she came, we changed our teachers as often as underwear!"

The Silversmith laughed.

"Morbrecia had become impossible," said Charm. "Wild. Rebellious. Uncontrollable. No one stayed more than a mede.* My mother appointed one governess after another and Morbrecia drove them

* *

* **Mede** – month. The Karisman calendar is divided into 13 medes

all mad. But Trum was different. She was strict but kind. Even Morbrecia liked her."

"And the doll?" prompted the Silversmith.

"Yes," said Charm. "I was coming to her. Trum allowed Morbrecia to bring Elmo to lessons. Morbrecia and I sat side by side, with Elmo in between. One day when Trum was writing on the board, I heard someone say 'Albina Trum is a magwort!'* It was MY voice. Though I swear it came from the doll."

"Quisto!" exclaimed the Silversmith.

"Morbrecia thought it was funny. Trum didn't. And I got into trouble," said Charm. "Another time Elmo jogged my elbow. I know it sounds ridiculous, but she *did*! She made me spill ink over my book.

When I said it was Elmo, Trum scolded me for telling lies. It was as if the doll was trying to get me into trouble."

The Silversmith sighed. She feared the doll possessed magical powers and was capable of malicious

* *

***Magwort** – probably the worst name you could call anyone! General term for a fool

mischief – or worse. She guessed it was influencing Morbrecia too.

"Anything else?" she asked.

Charm thought for a moment.

"There *was* an incident . . ." she began slowly. "Probably nothing, but it could have ended in disaster."

"What?" asked the Silversmith. "Please, go on."

"Well," said Charm, "one afternoon Morbrecia and I were on our own . . .

"I'm bored! Let's climb the tower. I've always wanted to go up there."

"No, we're not allowed. If anyone sees us, we'll be in trouble. And I'm afraid of heights."

"Oh, Charm! You're such a baby. If you're going to be queen of Karisma, you'd better start behaving like one. Come on, I'll race you to the top!"

"I didn't want Morbrecia to think I was a coward," Charm went on, "so I agreed. The tower was high and I was frightened. When we got to the top

Morbrecia insisted we went onto the battlements. I remember it was very windy that day. We could hardly stand up! There was a low wall and she dared me to look over the edge—"

Charm closed her eyes. She felt giddy, just thinking about it. "Morbrecia was behind me. As I took a step forward, a terrific gust of wind blew me against the wall."

The Silversmith gasped.

"There was a loose stone," said Charm, "and I felt it give way! Suddenly I found myself clawing at thin air. Morbrecia grabbed me and the stone went flying. It smashed to pieces in the courtyard. It could have been me—"

Charm faltered, reliving the awful incident.

"And," she said, her eyes meeting the Silversmith's, "the scariest part is yet to come."

"I can't imagine anything worse!" said the Silversmith.

"When we got back to our room," said Charm, "Elmo was sitting in a chair, grinning. In her lap lay a fragment of stone!"

Six

Sesame, Maddy and Gemma set off briskly across a field, in the direction of the sea. It was Yamir – one of the winter months in Karisma – and the girls felt chilly, dressed in their cool, summery clothes. As they walked, Sesame told Gemma about the stolen charm bracelet, and kept a sharp lookout for charms along the way.

"How many charms have you found?" asked Gemma, fascinated by Sesame's story.

"Three," replied Sesame. "The heart, horseshoe and shell. Ten are still missing. It's really important Queen Charm has them all back."

"I see why you're called Charmseekers," said Gemma. "It's a secret club, right?"

"Mm," said Maddy, who'd been unusually quiet. Listening to Sesame talking about Karisma, her cheeks flamed and her heartbeat quickened. She didn't want Gemma knowing so much. This was *her* secret with Ses! She knew she was being silly, but it had been something special she and Sesame had shared. They were best friends! When Gemma wasn't looking, she shot Sesame a meaningful look. "We said we wouldn't tell anyone."

"True—" began Sesame. She could tell Maddy was mad at her, but what could she do? Gemma was here. Their secret was out. Besides, she thought Maddy was being a bit unfair.

"Gemma's part of the quest now," she said. "She's a Charmseeker too."

Gemma looked pleased.

"Thanks," she said.

"Whatever," said Maddy moodily.

There was an awkward silence. Gemma was afraid they'd start quarrelling.

"If I hadn't come," she said, "I'd never have believed you about Karisma. It sounds too fantastic. I mean, how did we get here?"

Maddy shrugged.

"It happens," she said unhelpfully.

"When you're least expecting it," added Sesame.

Gemma looked worried. It had just dawned on her they were a world away from home.

"How do we get back?" she asked.

It was a question neither Sesame nor Maddy could begin to answer. Sesame tried to reassure her.

"Don't worry," she said, glancing back the way they had come. The weather was overcast and gloomy, with thick, grey clouds gathering out to sea. But Etok's gatehouse was huge. She reckoned they'd see it from miles away. "We just have to get to the gate on time."

And as she spoke, they heard the clock strike one.

By chance, Zorgan saw them arrive. He had been gazing into his crystal ball, when Sesame, Maddy and Gemma suddenly tumbled through the stars and fell into Karisma.

"Balam Outworlders!" he cursed. "Three of them

this time. Will Sesame Brown never give up? Well, she'll be sorry . . ."

For a while Zorgan stood stroking his pet bandrall,*

* *

* **Bandrall** – rare flying mammal, native to Karisma

Vanda, considering what to do. Soon he'd thought of an excellent idea and, after a few preparations, he summoned one of his pixies. Nix stood, awaiting orders.

"Take these," he said, handing her a packet of seeds.

"What are they, Master?" asked Nix.

"Magic Thorns," said Zorgan. "Scatter them at Cape Cat. They grow fast, so watch your wings! And do the job properly. My forest of thorns must prevent those Outworlders getting back to the gate."

"Yes, Master," said Nix. "Orders understood!"

The pixie flew off at lightning speed, eager to carry out her mission. Zorgan smirked as he watched her go. Soon Sesame Brown and her interfering friends would be trapped and at his mercy.

"Then," he said to Vanda, "I shall take great pleasure in getting rid of them!"

As an afterthought, he sent Vanda to spy on them.

Vanda knew the area well; the high cliffs around Cape Cat were traditional nesting places for bandralls. She would be his eyes and ears.

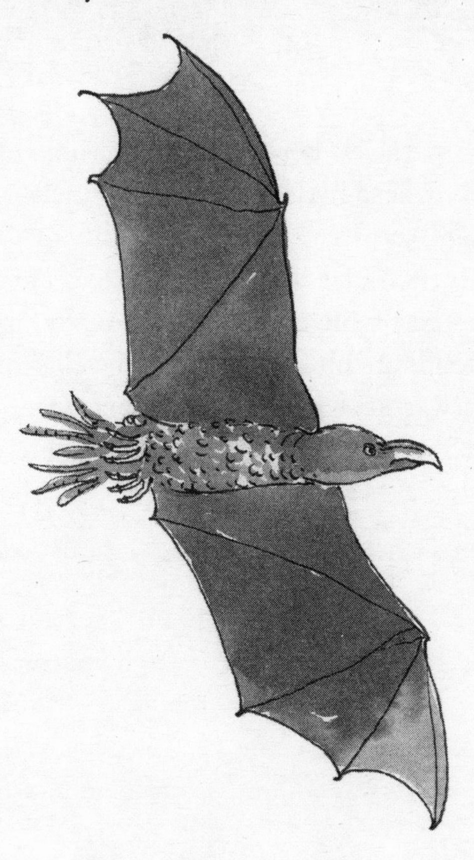

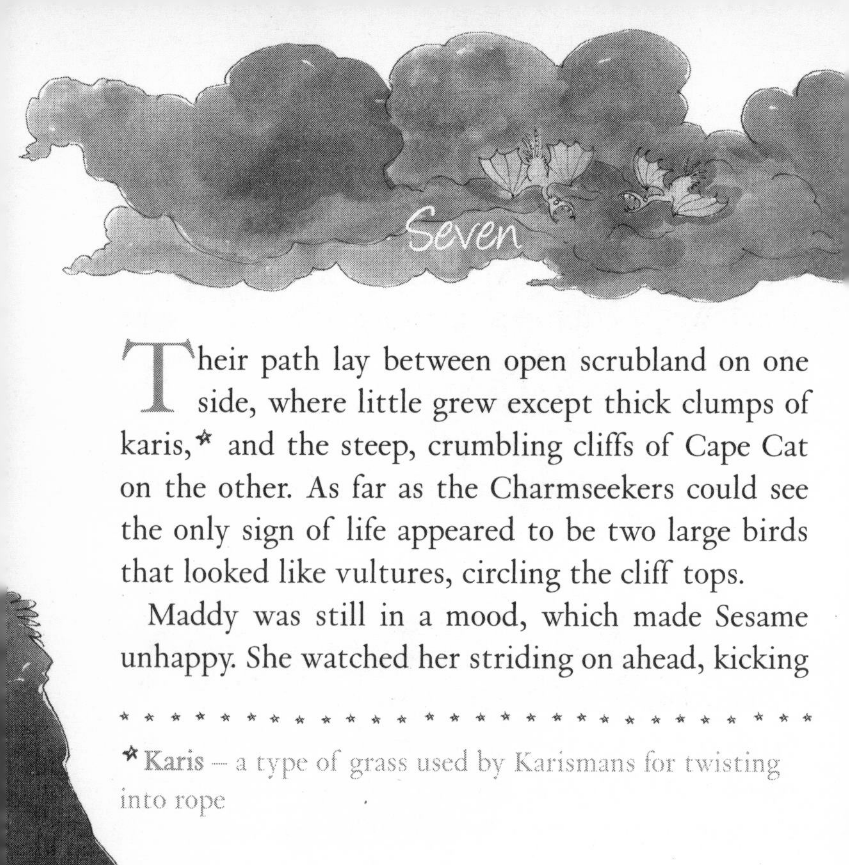

Seven

Their path lay between open scrubland on one side, where little grew except thick clumps of karis,* and the steep, crumbling cliffs of Cape Cat on the other. As far as the Charmseekers could see the only sign of life appeared to be two large birds that looked like vultures, circling the cliff tops.

Maddy was still in a mood, which made Sesame unhappy. She watched her striding on ahead, kicking

* *

* **Karis** – a type of grass used by Karismans for twisting into rope

at loose stones. Sesame fiddled with the friendship band that Gemma had made. It reminded her of how, only a short while ago, they were all having such fun together at the SuperDome. She wished it could be like that now. They were friends for ever, weren't they? We *have* to stick together, thought Sesame. We're Charmseekers. We're a team! Was there a reason all three of them had come? She remembered the weird feeling she'd had in the tree earlier, when she thought she was falling into Karisma. Maybe this time she would need her friends?

Crossly, Maddy kicked a large stone; it landed in a tuft of karis, and a startled swiftwing flew up from its nest.

"Oh, how pretty!" cried Sesame, delighted to see the bright green and crimson bird. Against the dull, wintry sky it was the only colourful thing in sight. Then, seeing its nest, she stopped to examine it with Gemma.

"Cool," said Gemma, admiring the way the bird had woven grass into a neat little ball.

"Maddy!" Sesame called. "Come here. Look!"

Thinking Sesame had found a charm Maddy, who'd gone ahead alone, spun round. The path ran perilously close to the cliff edge and, as she turned, a part of it crumbled away. A split second later, she fell.

"A-a-a-a-a-a-rh!"

screamed Maddy, flinging out her arms in a desperate attempt to steady herself. But it was no good. Sesame and Gemma watched in horror, as she tumbled down the cliff in an avalanche of debris.

"MADDY!" yelled Sesame, frantically peering through the dust.

Gemma bit her lip.

"I can't see her," she said anxiously.

For what seemed ages, everything was eerily quiet. Then suddenly they heard Maddy's voice, floating up to them from below:

"Help! I can't move!"

"I'm coming!" cried Sesame. And with no thought for her own safety, she scrambled down the rocky slope. She found Maddy lying on a ledge, halfway down the cliff.

"Oh, Ses," she moaned. "I've twisted my ankle."

"I'll soon have you out of here," said Sesame, sounding much more confident than she felt. She gave Gemma a quick wave, then turned again to Maddy.

"We need a rope," she said.

Maddy rolled her eyes.

"Like we're going to find one here," she said. "I suppose we could tie our friendship bands together! Sorry. Feeble joke—"

"No, that's brill!" said Sesame, her eyes shining. "You've given me an idea."

Her thoughts were racing. She remembered the bird's nest woven from grass. Maybe Gemma could plait grass like their wristbands to make a rope. She cupped her hands and shouted up to her:

"Grass . . . plait . . . rope!"

When Gemma looked puzzled, Sesame tapped her pink silky friendship band. Then she twigged.

"Got it!" cried Gemma, giving Sesame and Maddy the thumbs up. As she hurried off to pick grass, away in the distance she heard the clock strike two . . .

While Gemma was gathering grass, Nix was scattering seeds. Soon there would be a forest of thorn trees, to cut off the Charmseekers' escape!

Gemma sat cross-legged beside a huge pile of grass. Her fingers flew – over, under, over, under – deftly plaiting the karis and knotting the lengths together. She'd never worked so fast, and soon a

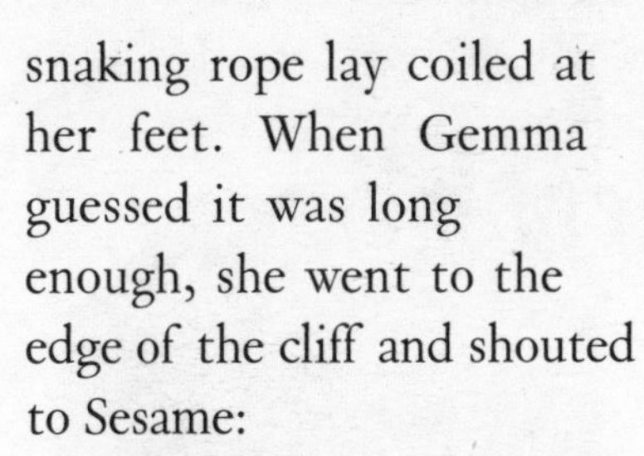

snaking rope lay coiled at her feet. When Gemma guessed it was long enough, she went to the edge of the cliff and shouted to Sesame:

"Here it comes. Catch!"

Holding tight to one end, she threw the rope down. Sesame caught it easily and wound a length round Maddy's waist, securing it with a knot. When Maddy gingerly stood on her injured foot, she winced:

"Ouch!"

"Oh, Maddy," said Sesame, helping her to stand. "Just hang on to the rope. Gemma will pull you up."

"Ready when you are!" cried Gemma, bracing herself to take the strain. Then, hand over hand, she slowly hauled Maddy upwards, until with one tremendous heave, Maddy crawled to safety.

"Phew!" she gasped. "Thanks, Gemma. You were awesome!"

Below on the ledge, Sesame was relieved to see Maddy smiling and waving. Now it was her turn. Gemma threw the rope down and Sesame gave it a quick tug, to let Gemma know she was ready. While Gemma held fast at the top, Sesame expertly climbed the rope as she'd been taught in P.E. at school.

She was doing well, until she was startled by a piercing

screeeech!

A vicious-looking bandrall flew out from a crevice, dived and pecked at her legs! Taken completely by surprise Sesame nearly let go of the rope, but somehow managed to cling on.

"Ow, ow!" yelped Sesame, aiming a kick. She missed and the bandrall prepared for another attack. Sesame was scared of the fiendish bird, but all she could think about was holding onto the rope and getting to the top. To make matters worse, she caught sight of another bird, which looked a lot like this one, circling overhead. Oh great, she thought. Its friend is about to have a go at me too!

"Ses!" shouted Maddy, watching helplessly from above. She could see Sesame swinging about wildly, trying to fend off another painful stab from the razor-sharp beak.

"Hold on!" cried Gemma, digging in her heels to steady herself. She was being pulled towards the edge of the cliff!

Seeing Gemma in danger, Maddy hopped over to her. Ignoring the pains shooting from her ankle, she clasped Gemma round the waist, closed her eyes and gritted her teeth. Then she hauled with all her strength, and eased Gemma back to the path.

"Thanks, Maddy," she said. "I thought I was going over!" Then to her horror, she suddenly felt the rope go slack . . .

"SESAME!" she yelled.

Below them on the cliff-face Sesame had swung herself over to a crack in the rock, and had wedged herself there. She hoped the horrid bird would go away, but it squawked furiously and flapped its wings. Then Sesame saw the reason why: she was standing in its nest!

Eight

Sharp twigs tore at her leggings. As Sesame stooped to untangle herself, a shaft of wintry sun pierced the gloom. It caught a bright, shiny object lying in the nest. A silvery glint. A flash! Twinkling specks of light danced in the sunbeams.

Sesame's necklace tingled. She reached between the scratchy sticks and felt her fingers close around something cool. When she looked, she saw it was a charm – a beautiful silver cat! She cradled it in her hand, momentarily forgetting the danger she was in. She had found another charm for the queen! Her thoughts were interrupted by Gemma and Maddy, frantically calling:

"What's happened? Are you okay?"

"Ses? Ses? SHOOO!"

Maddy directed the last word at Vanda, who was hovering above her and Gemma, taking a closer look.

"I've found another charm!" cried Sesame, putting it in her pocket as she edged out of the crevice. Just in time she shielded her face, as the first bandrall lunged. "Quick, Gemma, Maddy. Pull me up!"

Sesame gripped the rope with one hand, doing her best to protect herself with the other. Again and again the bandrall swooped to jab Sesame's legs with her beak. But as soon as Sesame reached the top, Vanda gave an angry squawk – and flew away.

Together again at last, the three girls flopped on the grass. Sesame dabbed at her sore legs with a handkerchief. Her silvery leggings were full of holes! But nothing could spoil her excitement at finding the cat. She took the little charm from her pocket and passed it round for the others to see. It was the first time Gemma had seen any of the charms.

"Oh, it's fab!" she said. "I'd love to see the others."

"Of course," said Sesame, putting the cat safely

away again. "I'll show you sometime. I promise. They're in my special jewellery box at home."

Maddy smiled.

"You were totally brill, Gemma," she said. "Ses and I would have been in mega-trouble without you."

"Yes," agreed Sesame. "And if you hadn't fallen down the cliff, Maddy, I might never had found the cat! So in a way we all helped find the charm. We were *meant* to be here together. I just knew it!"

"Hooray for us Charmseekers!" said Maddy.

And they all cheered. Then Vanda, who'd been watching them the whole time, flew off to Zorgan's Tower.

"Er, I don't want to spoil the fun," said Sesame, "but I think we should be getting back to the gate."

"You're right," said Gemma, jumping up. "I heard the clock strike two *ages* ago!"

Sesame helped Maddy to her feet and looked concerned, as she watched her limp around.

"I can't walk very fast," said Maddy apologetically. "I'll slow you down."

"You can hold onto us," chorused Sesame and Gemma.

They started back along the path, but very soon noticed that nothing looked the same. Where once there had been sparse scrubland, now thick thorn bushes grew. And they appeared to be *growing*!

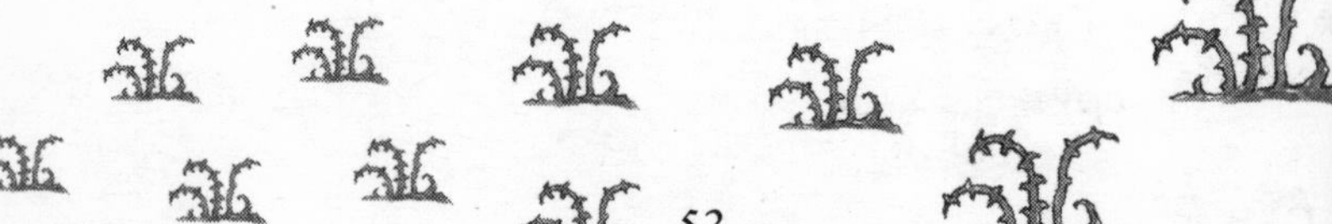

On one of them, Sesame spotted a small paper packet caught in the branches. Her sharp eyes didn't miss a thing. She stopped to unhook it, then read the writing on the pack:

Zorgan's
MAGIC
SEEDS
For best results,
sprinkle seeds over
rough ground and
watch them GROW!

"Hm, Zorgan?" said Sesame thoughtfully. "I'm sure Hob mentioned him once. When I first came to Karisma."

"And Hob told us about his two pixies, remember?" said Maddy. "We escaped from one of them at Morbrecia's castle. Nasty little thing! She threatened us with cobwebby stuff."

"—and tried to take the horseshoe charm!" said Sesame. "Maybe she dropped this? Perhaps Zorgan sent her here?"

Gemma was looking more and more bewildered.

"Zorgan? Hob? Morbrecia? Who are they all?" she asked.

"Tell you as we go," said Sesame, anxious to keep going. "Zorgan's Magic Thorns are growing like mad!"

It was true. The ground was now covered with shrubs bristling with thorns. And they were getting bigger by the minute. Sesame tried to get her bearings.

"Can anyone see Etok's gatehouse?" she said. "It's enormous. We should be able to see it."

"Are you sure this is the right way?" asked Gemma. She sounded panicky.

"It must be," said Maddy. "The sea was definitely on our left when we came. Now it's on our right."

"There!" cried Sesame, suddenly spotting the gatehouse tower in the distance. She felt afraid. Her throat was dry. "Come on," she said. "We must find a way to the gate!"

And as they set off again, the clock struck three.

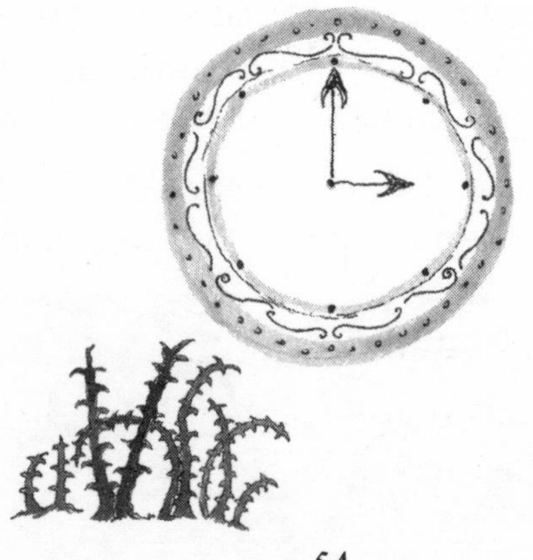

Nine

The Silversmith was shocked. For a while she sat reflecting on all that Charm had said. It was worse than she feared. So, Morbrecia's doll had supernatural powers, had she? The fragment of stone was proof enough of that. At length, Charm's firm but gentle voice broke in:

"So what is to be done about my sister?"

"Well, Your Majesty," said the Silversmith. "I understand Morbrecia better, after all you've told me this afternoon. Thank you. I've long suspected she stole your bracelet, though I'm also convinced Zorgan was behind that plot. But it's clear Elmo is influencing her too! I'm afraid Morbrecia will try anything to prevent Sesame finding your charms. Zorgan too. But Sesame *will* find them, you may be sure of that! She won't give up. Until then, she will be in constant danger."

"I'll do whatever I can to protect her," promised Charm. "I'll appoint Officer Dork as her personal bodyguard and—"

The Silversmith smiled and raised her hand.

"With respect, Your Majesty, that won't work. Sesame is a Charmseeker. She has to meet this challenge on her own, whatever dangers lie in her path. But as for Morbrecia . . ." The Silversmith paused, choosing her words carefully. After all, she was the queen's sister. "Perhaps Officer Dork could keep an eye on her from now on? He's your most trusted guard. If Dork should report any wrongdoings against you or the Charmseekers, you would have proof of Morbrecia's treachery. Then you could act accordingly."

"How wise you are!" said Charm. "That is exactly what I shall do. I'm afraid that still leaves the problem of Zorgan, though."

"Yes," said the Silversmith gravely. "He is quite another matter. We can only hope Sesame comes to no harm when next she comes to Karisma!"

* * * *

Vanda returned to Zorgan with news that Sesame had found another charm. In his wildest dreams Zorgan could not have imagined Sesame would find one in a bandrall's nest! He rubbed his hands in gleeful anticipation. What luck! he thought. If Nix has done her job properly, I'll have Sesame snared and a charm in the bargain! He wasted no time in summoning Dina.

"Stand by for orders," he commanded.

"Yes, Master," said Dina, eager for action.

Zorgan peered into his crystal ball to

focus on Nix. It seemed that the thorn seeds she'd scattered had grown into an impenetrable forest.

"Spallah!"* he exclaimed. "Nix has done well. Ha ha! Now I'll cast a mist of Timeless Sleep over the Charmseekers. And they shall be no more. Go now, Dina. Fetch my prize. I *will* have that charm!"

Meanwhile, back at the gatehouse, Etok had been waiting for the Charmseekers to return. Time was ticking away. Only ten minutes to go before the gate shut and he would be powerless to let them through. He was a gatekeeper. Rules were rules.

Stepping outside, Etok was amazed to find himself surrounded by prickly trees. He'd never seen anything like them. Etok was concerned for the safety of Sesame Brown and her friends. They'd come to search for the queen's missing charms and it was his duty to protect them, if he could. Besides, the Charmseekers had helped him and one good turn deserved another!

* **Spallah** – excellent! A triumphant expression

The giant gatekeeper could see over even the tallest thorn trees, so he took a good look round for the girls . . .

"Ouch!" cried Sesame, for the umpteenth time, untangling her hair from a thorny branch. She was leading the way to the gatehouse. "Here, I've found another gap."

The three girls had been making slow but steady progress, battling their way towards the gate. Little did they know it, but they were so nearly there! Fortunately for the Charmseekers, Nix had scattered the seeds carelessly, leaving gaps between the thorns for them to squeeze through. Maddy was doing her best, hopping between Sesame and Gemma. But it was taking time, and all too soon they heard the clock strike the first stroke of four.

Then out of nowhere came a strange, green mist.

Cloudy, evil-smelling vapour drifted through the forest, making them splutter and cough. Zorgan had cast a spell and filled the air with deadly Timeless Sleep.

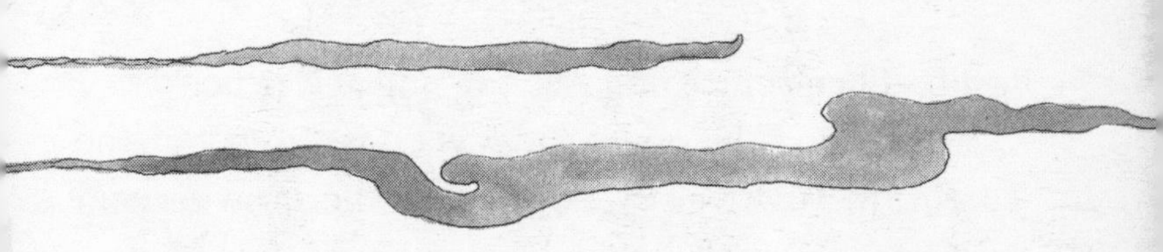

"Ugh!" exclaimed Maddy, holding her nose.

"Yuck!" cried Gemma, choking.

"I can't breathe!" Sesame gasped, fighting for air.

Her head was spinning. Her ears were ringing. She was losing consciousness. She reached out for Maddy and Gemma. Far away she heard the clock strike

again. Then something was tugging at her pocket.

It was Dina the pixie! She was trying to get at the charm. Instinctively Sesame swung her arm to fend off Dina. But she was weak, so weak . . .

Sesame felt herself drifting. She couldn't tell whether she was falling or floating. She thought she heard someone call her name. SESAME! SESAME! And suddenly she was being lifted up, up, up through the swirling clouds of green . . .

"Just in time," said Etok, gently placing the girls

by the gate. "Setfair,* Charmseekers! Now GO!"

And on the very last stroke of four, they fell into a thousand stars.

* *

* **Setfair** – goodbye and good luck

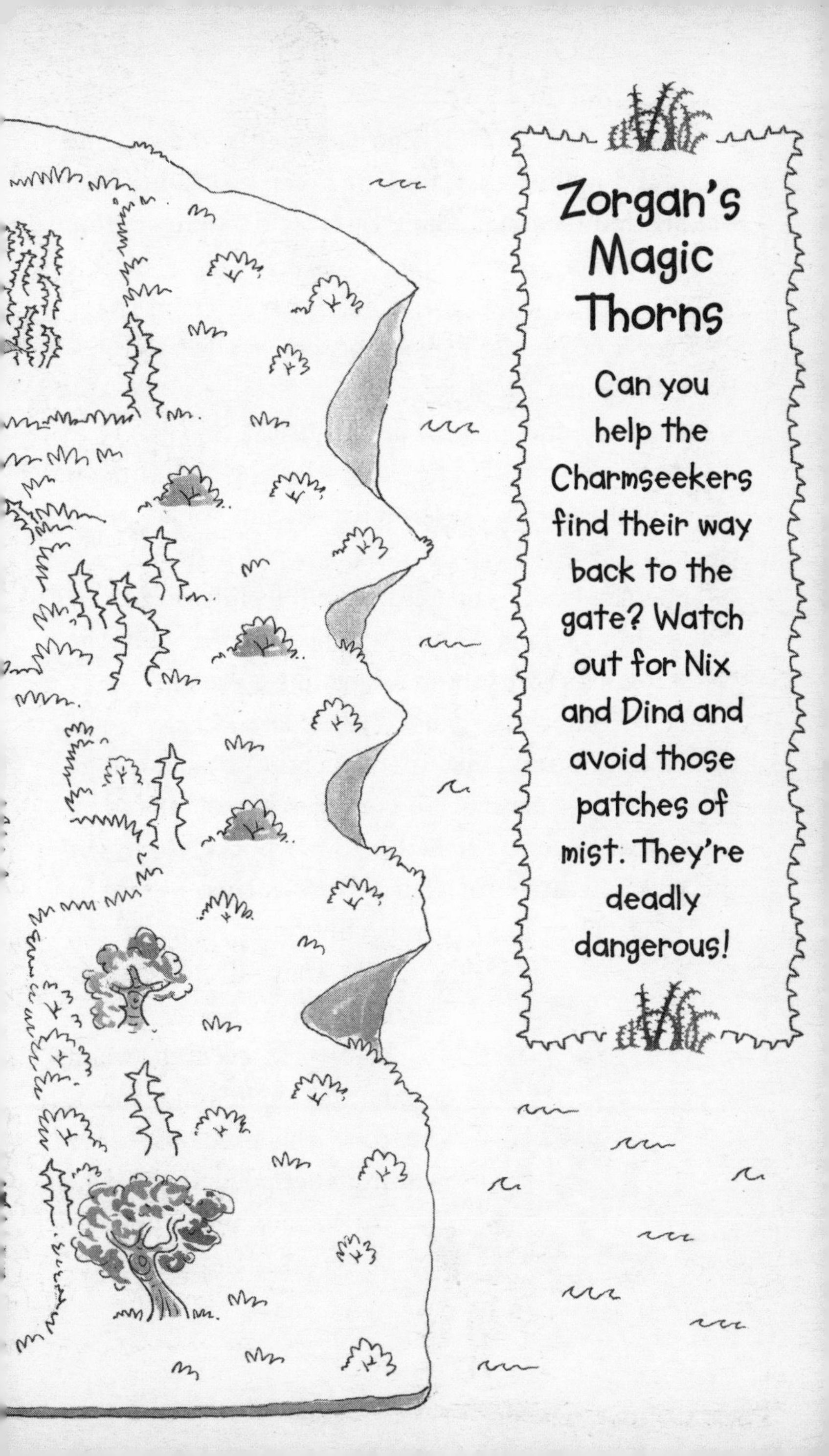
Zorgan's Magic Thorns
Can you help the Charmseekers find their way back to the gate? Watch out for Nix and Dina and avoid those patches of mist. They're deadly dangerous!

"GO! . . . go!"

Sesame blinked. Her head was still spinning. She was standing in a mist, under a green spotlight, with Maddy and Gemma. The Crystal Chix were smiling at them saying:

"Sorry girls, we've got to go. Show starts in five!"

"Bye," said Nic. "Thanks. Got some really good pics. Be in the paper tomorrow."

He turned and grinned at the girls.

"Here, take a look," he said, selecting a picture on his digital camera. "Sesame Brown and friends with the stars!"

"Thanks, Dad," said Sesame still feeling dizzy, but giving him a hug. "I can't believe we've met the Crystal Chix. Everything seems like a dream!"

The three girls exchanged bewildered glances, but this was not the time to talk about their strange adventure in Karisma. To convince herself it *had* all happened, Sesame reached into her pocket to finger the precious little cat charm. It was there – real as anything. Then her dad was chivvying them off the stage, and they all took their seats for the concert.

Later that evening, when Sesame was alone in her room, she took the precious silver cat from her pocket. She held it for a while, admiring every little detail: its arched back, long whiskers and slanting eyes. It was charming! Then she placed it carefully in her jewellery box. She wished Maddy and Gemma were with her to see the four charms safely in place beside the bracelet; the heart, the horseshoe, the shell and the cat.

"Nine more charms to find," she whispered to her teddy, Alfie. Then she closed the lid. "I must go back to Karisma soon!"

Sesame lay in bed thinking about some of the amazing things that had happened. It had been fabulous meeting the Crystal Chix. And she had a picture to prove it! But who would believe her about Karisma? Apart from finding another charm, which was *most* important, neither she, Maddy nor Gemma had much to show for the dangers they'd faced. Luckily Maddy's ankle was only slightly bruised, Gemma had chipped a fingernail and, curiously, Sesame had only one small hole in her leggings; somehow all the others had mysteriously disappeared. And they'd all survived that choking green mist!

Suddenly her eyelids felt very heavy. Sesame sighed

contentedly. There would be plenty to talk about with her friends tomorrow . . .

And when Nic popped in to say goodnight, he found Sesame sound asleep.

Ten

The Silversmith has had much to think about since her conversation with Charm. Now, more than ever, she wishes the thirteen charms could be together again and in Charm's possession.

Patience! she tells herself. That day will come, as surely as the two moons shine above Karisma. Until then, she must be vigilant and do everything in her power to help Sesame, whenever and wherever she can. But so many pitfalls and dangers lie ahead! Only Quilla, with her knowledge of the future, can say what might happen. Though perhaps knowing the future is not such a good thing. Look what had happened between Charm and Morbrecia! The Silversmith understood the reason for Morbrecia's jealousy, but once again the cause of all the trouble had been Zorgan. Oh, that she could find a way to deal with *him*!

Such negative thoughts are quickly set aside as the Silversmith sees another magic candle has gone out.

She claps her hands with joy. Sesame has found the cat! The beautiful silver cat. A tell-tale wisp of smoke spirals up from the candle that bears its name. Now

nine candles remain burning, nine glowing beacons of hope for their charms yet to be found.

Meanwhile Karisma remains in a state of chaos. The winds have changed. The exquisite golden butterflies of the south can no longer fly, to pollinate the clover fields of the north. Ah, but that is another story. It must be told another day!

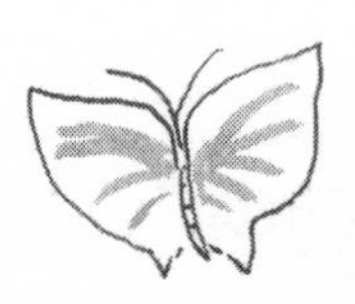

Acknowledgments

I owe a debt of gratitude to all those who have worked behind the scenes at Orion Children's Books and beyond to bring the *Charmseekers* books and their thirteen delightful charms to you. Since it would take more space than this edition allows to mention individuals by name, suffice it to say that I'm hugely grateful to my publishers and everyone involved with the publication of this series. In particular, my special thanks go to: my publisher, Fiona Kennedy, for her faith in believing I could write way beyond my own expectations. Her creative, tactful and skilful editing kept Sesame Brown on the right track and helped me to write a better story; my agent, Rosemary Sandberg; Jenny Glencross and Jane Hughes (Editorial); Alex Nicholas and Helen Speedy (Rights) Loulou Clark and Helen Ewing (Design); Clare Hennessy (Production); Jessica Killingley and Jo Dawson (Marketing); Pandora White (Orion Audio Books); Imogen Adams (Website designer – www.hammerinheels.com); Neil Pymer, the *real* Spinner Shindigs, for kind permission to use his name; and last, but by no means least, a million thanks go to my husband Tom for his inexhaustible patience, critical appraisal and support along the way.

Georgie Adams